To: Henry

To those who will go on holding tight to
their child-like wonder, burning desire to
question everything, and unquenchable
thirst for knowledge and understanding.

You are the future.

www.mascotbooks.com

Willow the Water Bear

For more information, please contact:
Mascot Books
620 Herndon Parkway #320
Herndon, VA 20170
info@mascotbooks.com

Library of Congress Control Number: 2017912651

CPSIA Code: PBANG1117A
ISBN-13: 978-1-68401-311-1

Printed in the United States

Willow the Water Bear

Written by HOUSTON T. KIDD Illustrated by ERIC L. BATES

Willow the Water Bear was a curious little thing.

But she wanted to do more than dance and sing.

"I wish I was a superhero!" Willow exclaimed.
"I'd save people and everyone would know my name!"

"You're perfectly fine!" Mr. Tardi declared.
"But I want to be strong," Willow shared.

"What if I told you," Mrs. Grade declared aloud,
"that you're already a superhero? Be proud!"

"I'm nothing special," Willow said with a sigh.
"Not special at all. I can't even fly."

Mr. Tardi stood up and held out eight hands.
Mrs. Grade did as well, as if it were planned.

"Come with us, Willow!" they both said politely.
"We'll show you a superhero. Hold on tightly!"

So away they went, through the forest of trees,
to the depths of the ocean, where the pressure squeezed.

"Amazing," shouted Willow. "But where's the superhero?"
"He's moved," said a sea clam. "Try looking near absolute zero."

"Near absolute zero?" a confused Willow replied.
"That's right," said the sea clam.
"Nice meeting you, goodbye!"

Their adventure continued to the chilly Antarctic Ocean,
where they met Mr. Krill, who approached them with caution.

"What brings you out here?" Mr. Krill whispered quietly.
"We're looking for a superhero!" Willow stated quite mightily.

"I'm afraid he's not here; in fact, you just missed him.
He's left planet Earth, but he's still in the Solar System."

"Left planet Earth?!" Willow shouted with fear.
"No worries," said Mrs. Grade. "Follow us, my dear."

Scared but excited, Willow followed the two.
"What is that?" Willow asked. "Oh wait, that's the Moon!"

They arrived on the Moon in the vacuum of space.
Surely THIS must be where the hero awaits!?

"Jo? Laz? What are you two doing here?
Have you seen the superhero?" Willow asked, full of cheer.

"We're traveling with our family for a week on vacation.
No superheroes here, just rest and relaxation."

"I want to go home," Willow the Water Bear cried.
"There's no such thing as superheroes. Admit it, you lied!"

"We did not lie," Mr. Tardi said sharply.
"That's true," said Mrs. Grade. "You accuse us falsely."

"Think about it Willow," she said with a grin.
"What if all along the hero was within?"

"You've traveled the world and the depths of the ocean,
to the chill of the Antarctic where most life lacks motion."

"Just look where you stand in the vacuum of space.
Name one other creature who could survive in this place.

Have you figured it out? Is it all becoming clearer?
Superheroes ARE real! Just look in the mirror!"

10 TARDIGRADE (WATER BEAR) FACTS WITH DR. THOMAS C. BOOTHBY – *Biologist*

1. Tardigrades can be found almost everywhere and live on every continent, including Antarctica.

2. They were first discovered by Johann August Ephraim Goeze in 1773 and were given their name by Lazzaro Spallanzani in 1776.

3. Tardigrades are incredibly unique because they can survive stresses that are beyond extreme, such as drying out, freezing, high temperatures, intense radiation, and even the vacuum of outer space.

4. They make up an entire group of tiny animals unto themselves, and are most closely related to arthropods (which include things like insects and crustaceans) and nematodes (microscopic round worms).

5. Researchers believe that the common ancestor of tardigrades and their relatives was made up of additional parts (segments) and that tardigrades lost many of these middle segments. This basically makes them heads with legs.

6. Many people think there is only one kind of tardigrade, but scientists have actually discovered over 1,200 different species and counting.

7. All tardigrades have a tough cuticle or exoskeleton surrounding them. Some species have very ornate spikes, plates, and horns decorating their cuticle. Researchers believe these may help the tardigrades sense things about their environment.

8. Researchers also speculate that when tardigrades dry out, which is called the "tun" state, they can be picked up by the wind and carried around the world. This might help explain how they are so well distributed.

9. When hydrated, tardigrades rarely live for more than a few months. However, when dried or frozen, they can survive for years or, in some cases, decades.

10. If you have a microscope, you can find tardigrades living in your backyard, school playground, or local park.

For instructions on how to find your very own water bears, visit my website at tardigradehunters.weebly.com

Houston T. Kidd was born in South Hill, Virginia. A decorated United States Navy veteran, he served four years active duty and continues to serve in the reserves. Chasing a childhood dream, he went on to work in the film industry as a stand-in and stunt double for National Geographic and AMC Network productions before settling down on the outskirts of Research Triangle Park in North Carolina. He believes diversity and inclusion to be the spice of life and hopes that *Willow the Water Bear* will foster a love for science and inspire young minds to pursue their dreams!

MASCOT
BOOKS